nickelodeon

ni hao, kai-lan

Make a Splash!

Adapted by Geof Smith

Based on the teleplay "Rain or Shine" by Bradley Zweig

Illustrated by Jason Fruchter

A GOLDEN BOOK • NEW YORK

Library of Congress Control Number: 2009942238
ISBN: 978-0-375-87238-9
Printed in the United States of America
10 9 8 7 6 5 4 3 2

Ni hao! I'm Kai-lan!

I'm so happy it's a sunny day, because my friends and I are going to play outside. Do you like to play outside?

Super! We can all play together.

Look! It's YeYe. He likes
sunny weather, too. That's
when he works in his garden.

Here come Rintoo, Tolee, and Hoho. They're ready to play in the park.

Rintoo loves riding his bike really fast!

Tolee is an awesome skater!

Look how high Hoho's kite is!

I like spinning flowers up into the sky.

YeYe brought us raincoats and boots to keep us dry. *Xie xie*, YeYe.

I think Hoho got the wrong raincoat.

Rintoo, Tolee, and
Hoho don't like the rain.
They wanted to play in the park.
Now they think the day is ruined.

I think there are lots of super things to do in the rain.

You can catch raindrops on your nose . . .

and splash, splash, splash in puddles!

Do you think our friends are sad because they can't play with their toys in the rain? I think so, too.

We have to find a way to make them happy.

Look, it's YeYe! Do you think he's sad because he can't work in his garden while it rains? Let's ask him.

YeYe says he was a little sad at first, but then he remembered that he likes to see all the animals that come out in the rain.

Look! There are two snails.

Those worms are dancing in the rain.

Here comes
a turtle.

And there goes a frog!

I know what will make Rintoo, Tolee, and Hoho happy! They have to think about what they *can* do in the rain, not what they *can't* do. Let's go tell them so we can all play together.

We can't play the games we wanted to play, but maybe we can find new ones.

Look! Those snails are giving each other rides on a sled. Do you think they will give Tolee a ride?

Hooray! The snails are pulling Tolee, and he's having a great time. To help the snails, say *pull* in Chinese. *La!*

That frog is sliding pretty fast. Do you think Rintoo and Hoho could slide on a big leaf, too?

Look at Rintoo and Hoho go, go, go!

Even Mr. Sun has come out to play. He wants to show us something special he can do in the rain.

Mr. Sun made a rainbow!

Even though it rained, it was a super awesome day. I'm so glad you helped our friends find new things to do. You make my heart feel super happy. Goodbye! *Zai jian!*